YOUR SPECIAL STAR

Jessica M. Collette

Illustrated By Mary Manning

outskirtspress
DENVER, COLORADO

For:

Joshua Ryan Collette—My Special Star

Forever, your light shines brightly.

Today was the hardest day of Bobby's life. He stood by his dad, as relatives and others he did not know, said they were sorry for his mom's passing. They spoke about how wonderful his mom HAD been. All Bobby could think, was he did not want to say good-bye to her.

Bobby's dad leaned toward his son and whispered in his ear, "Mom left you something. It will be waiting for you on your bed." Dad and son locked sad eyes together, but in the moment, Bobby's eyes sparkled with a glimmer of hope.

After all guests had left, Bobby eagerly opened the door to his bedroom. His eyes fixed upon a rolled up object tied with a golden rope and tassels. As Bobby grasped the scroll and gently began to unroll it, he saw his mom's handwriting and began to read aloud, "Love from above." Choking back tears, Bobby stopped reading aloud and continued silently.

As he reached the end and fixed his eyes on the words, *With eternal love from above, Mom,* a single tear left Bobby's eye and dropped onto the parchment, directly on top of the word *Mom.* Grateful for this gift, Bobby gently rolled up the scroll and held it to his chest as he fell asleep.

As Bobby slept, his dreams were alive with images of his mom and the many fun times they shared together.

Upon waking, Bobby knew exactly what his mom intended for him to do with the scroll—it was meant to be shared!

When Bobby heard Mrs. Cole's husband had passed, he knocked on her door. When Mrs. Cole answered, Bobby did not say he was sorry, but instead began to read his mom's scroll aloud to her, "Love from above."

He left Mrs. Cole with a copy he had handwritten himself. The only addition Bobby added was, *April 12—Little Pond Park.*

When Bobby heard Mr. and Mrs. Smith's baby had not come home with them from the hospital, he alsoreadthemthescroll. They thanked him for the handwritten copy and acknowledged the date at the park.

When Bobby heard his friend John's dog had passed, he shared the scroll with him. He gave him a handwritten copy and encouraged John to remember the date at the park.

Bobby made many visits to his neighbors, sharing the scroll with each who had experienced the passing of a loved one. He provided handwritten copies to them all, encouraging each one to take note of the date at the park.

As April 12 arrived, Bobby gathered items to take with him. He chose a blanket, a sweatshirt, some snacks, the telescope, and his mom's scroll, which he carefully secured around his neck. His dad joined him on the walk toward the park.

As they made their way through the park gates, his dad said, "It is going to be a perfect night, Bobby. Not a cloud in the sky!"

Rounding the corner to the open field, Bobby did not hear anyone.

"It will probably be just you and me," Bobby said to his dad as he lowered his head.

Looking up to find the right spot on the grass, Bobby was amazed to see a large gathering of people. Not only did he see Mrs. Cole, Mr. and Mrs. Smith and John, but many, many others. Seeing Bobby, they all stood and began to applaud him.

Bobby made his way to the front of the crowd, setting his items down and pointing his telescope toward the night sky. As he thanked everyone for coming, Bobby removed his mom's scroll from around his neck and slowly unrolled it.

Bobby cleared his throat, "Please feel free to say this aloud with me. You can add your loved one's name at the end where my mom signed hers."

Dear Bobby,

Love from above; I'm your special star;
I'm glad to see just how you are;

I gaze upon you from my star shaped window;
A witness to how all your days go;

Even when you feel upset and miss me so badly;
Please take comfort knowing I watch you gladly;

Forever my light shines on you brightly;
Love from above, I will send to you nightly.

With eternal love from above,
Mom

As Bobby finished reading the scroll, he was amazed to see the spot where his tear had fallen on his mom's signature. His tear and the ink had mixed, spreading to make the shape of a star. Bobby smiled at the wonder of this and then addressed the crowd.

Pointing to the night sky, telescope in hand, Bobby enthusiastically said, "Let's all find our special star."

Little Pond Park became a regular gathering spot. At those gatherings, Bobby proved how wonderful his mom IS, by passing on the legacy of her scroll.

As each gathering got larger, more and more shared the story of their special star. They laughed; they cried and ultimately made new memories together, during those starry nights in Little Pond Park.

Dear _____,
    (Your name)

Love from above; I'm your special star;
I'm glad to see just how you are;

I gaze upon you from my star shaped window;
A witness to how all your days go;

Even when you feel upset and miss me so badly;
Please take comfort knowing I watch you gladly;

Forever my light shines on you brightly;
Love from above, I will send to you nightly.

With eternal love from above,

_____

(Your special star's name)

CPSIA information can be obtained at www.ICGtesting.com
Printed in the USA
BVIW12n0401301017
498980BV00011B/117